Moonstone Landing

by

Meara Platt

Dragonblade Publishing, Inc. is an imprint of Kathryn Le Veque Novels, Inc.
P.O. Box 23
Moreno Valley, CA 92556
ceo@dragonbladepublishing.com

Produced in the United States of America

First Edition September 2022
Print Edition

ARE YOU SIGNED UP FOR DRAGONBLADE'S BLOG?

You'll get the latest news and information on exclusive giveaways, exclusive excerpts, coming releases, sales, free books, cover reveals and more.

Check out our complete list of authors, too!

No spam, no junk. That's a promise!

Sign Up Here

www.dragonbladepublishing.com

Dearest Reader;

Thank you for your support of a small press. At Dragonblade Publishing, we strive to bring you the highest quality Historical Romance from some of the best authors in the business. Without your support, there is no 'us', so we sincerely hope you adore these stories and find some new favorite authors along the way.

Happy Reading!

CEO, Dragonblade Publishing

Additional Dragonblade books by
Author Meara Platt

The Moonstone Landing Series
Moonstone Landing

The Book of Love Series
The Look of Love
The Touch of Love
The Taste of Love
The Song of Love
The Scent of Love
The Kiss of Love
The Chance of Love
The Gift of Love
The Heart of Love
The Hope of Love (novella)
The Promise of Love
The Wonder of Love
The Journey of Love
The Dream of Love (novella)
The Treasure of Love
The Dance of Love
The Miracle of Love
The Remembrance of Love (novella)

Dark Gardens Series
Garden of Shadows
Garden of Light
Garden of Dragons
Garden of Destiny
Garden of Angels

The Farthingale Series

If You Wished For Me (A Novella)

The Lyon's Den Connected World

Kiss of the Lyon

The Lyon's Surprise

Lyon in the Rough

Pirates of Britannia Series

Pearls of Fire

De Wolfe Pack: The Series

Nobody's Angel

Kiss an Angel

Bhrodi's Angel

Also from Meara Platt

Aislin

All I Want for Christmas

Chapter One

Moonstone Landing
Cornwall, England
July 1805

"OF ALL THE gall," Lady Henleigh Killigrew muttered as the same man she had seen walking out of the early morning mist these past three days was here again, about to cross her garden with the arrogant air of someone who belonged.

But he did not belong here.

He did not own her garden or her newly acquired residence, Moonstone Cottage, to which the charming garden was attached.

"You, there!" she called out to him as he strode up the cliff steps toward her home. The steps led down onto a small sand beach that also belonged to her now. "Who are you and what are you doing on my property?"

He pretended not to hear her and simply continued to march along the flowered path. She would not mind so much if he were properly dressed. But this knave was wearing nothing but his breeches and boots, his shirt of an obviously fine white lawn material slung over his shoulder. No doubt he had gone for a dawn swim, for his dark hair was slicked back and damp curls clung to his neck. Water droplets gleamed across his firm, tanned chest.

He probably assumed she would be asleep at this early hour and thought he could impose with impunity.

"Sir!" She drew her robe tight over her nightrail and leaned over the balcony of her upper-story bedchamber, hoping to attract his attention before he disappeared around the side of the house. She had no idea who he was or where he went each morning. Perhaps it was to the nearby woods or down the lane toward the village of Moonstone Landing, although yesterday she had scrambled from window to window trying to spot him, to no avail.

If only he weren't so arrogant about trespassing on her property.

If only he would put his shirt on instead of striding across her grounds with it casually slung over his shoulder, as though he hadn't a care in the world.

She donned her slippers, grabbed the hunting rifle she kept by the side of her bed, and hurried downstairs to the front door. Perhaps it was a foolish thing to do, for she lived here alone, and the small day staff she maintained was not due to arrive for several hours yet.

Since the cottage was a new purchase for her, she had immediately hired a cook, maid, and groundskeeper earlier this week, but none of them would agree to sleep in because of some nonsense about a ghost in residence at Moonstone Cottage or some such foolish legend.

Well, she hadn't seen a ghost, only this impudent gentleman.

She knew for certain he was a gentleman because his clothes, the little he had on, were too fine for a working man, although his body was surprisingly well-honed for a man of leisure.

The sun was beginning to burn away the mist, but smoky wisps of gray remained swirling about her legs as she hurried out of the cottage in search of him. The air was cool at this early hour and carried the scent of dew and salt from the nearby English Channel. "Blast it. Where did you go, you sneaky fellow?"

She walked around the house but saw no one anywhere, not a soul walking toward the woods or down the lane into town.

Several squirrels stared at her as she returned to the garden where she had first noticed him. Birds began to chirp amid the lush foliage, probably gossiping about the mad young woman running around in her nightclothes and toting a rifle she had never used before. She frowned up at the treetops to address the birds. "How hard can it be to shoot this thing? Just aim and fire."

The birds eerily quieted.

She shook her head and walked to the flower beds on her way toward the cliff steps.

This area of Cornwall was known for its red stone cliffs and beautiful beaches, as well as its warm weather. Moonstone Cottage included ownership of a slight stretch of both cliffs and beach.

She gripped the sturdy wooden railing and peered over the red stone heights to the sandy beach below on the chance the trespasser had returned the way he came. But the beach was barren save for a few birds hovering over the mist-covered waves in search of fish.

The wind carried the sound of those waves gently lapping the shore. "This is maddening."

What sort of man goes swimming in dark waters anyway?

The sun had not quite yet burned through the mist, so those wispy gray tendrils still hovered over patches of the water like so many silent ghosts.

A shiver ran up Henleigh's spine.

She turned suddenly, sensing someone was close. She had felt an icy breath upon her neck. But when she turned, no one was there.

Is this why the birds had stopped chirping? The squirrels earlier scampering in her garden were now frozen in place, as though turned to stone.

She stepped back from the cliff face and hurried back inside the house, shutting the door behind her and latching it securely. Then she realized the stranger might have crept inside the house while she was outside chasing him.

"Calm yourself, Hen," she whispered, clutching the rifle a little tighter as she hurried upstairs to her bedchamber and latched that door behind her as well.

She glanced around, realizing she might now have locked herself in with the stranger. "I have a loaded rifle," she warned, kneeling down to peer under her bed. It was a big, masculine-looking thing with a dark wood headboard and footboard etched with what looked like sea serpents on them and a square canopy over the top draped in a heavy, ocean blue damask.

All the furniture and furnishings in this bedchamber and throughout the cottage had a masculine, nautical feel. The outside did, too. The stone had been painted white, and the shutters were all of a nautical blue, but the cottage's appearance was softened by the abundance of red roses in front and the beautiful sweep of roses and colorful wildflowers around back.

She had fallen in love with the place at first sight and knew she had to have it when shown through the captain's bedchamber to the balcony and its overlook onto the garden and beyond to the sea.

"Dust balls," she muttered, squinting as she peered under the bed and spotted a few. She would ask Marjorie to sweep under there as soon as she arrived for work, but that would not be for a few hours yet.

With rifle still firmly in hand, she yanked open the door to her wardrobe. Her clothes were just as she had left them, her gowns neatly arranged by color and her delicate unmentionables undisturbed. She breathed a sigh of relief, for there was no place else within the room where the bounder could hide.

Unless he is hiding on the balcony.

She cautiously poked her head out and saw no one. "Oh, thank goodness."

Her nerves had gotten the better of her, causing her to imagine this stranger leaping out at her in places he was not.

She set her rifle back in its spot beside her bed and walked over to one of the plump chairs set beside the fireplace. She sank down on it, for her hands were trembling, and her heart was racing so that she could hardly catch her breath.

She closed her eyes a moment to steady herself. "No one here. You are safe, Hen."

"What sort of name is Hen?" A man's deep voice came from behind her, his words coming out in a soft growl.

She gasped and shot to her feet, immediately wanting to grab for her rifle and realizing she had left it by her bed.

Stupid.

Stupid.

Why did she ever let it out of her hands?

However, she put on a brave face for this stranger, unwilling to show him how frightened she truly was. "Who are you and...what...are you...doing..."

Drat!

Her heart was now in a fast flutter, and she could not catch her breath. How did he get in? Her door was latched. She had checked every possible hiding spot. "This is...my...chamber..."

He growled softly again. "You dare to call it yours?"

The prior owner had been a sea captain. "Indeed, I do. I simply have not started redecorating it yet. That project will start next month."

"Over my dead—" The very stranger she had seen outside earlier was now standing before her with his shirt still off, and glowering at her. His massive chest blocked her view of the rifle.

Lord, he was big.

His arms bulged with muscles as he crossed them over his chest, but his body was taut, lean, and finely rippled.

His eyes were the deepest blue she had ever seen.

He was handsome, even for a man who was about to kill her. However, he made no attempt to reach for her, just stood angrily staring at her.

Was he going to kill her?

She foolishly asked him the question, too late realizing she might have put the idea in his head when he likely only meant to frighten her or steal from her.

Yes, perhaps he was a thief.

A well-dressed one, if the cut of his breeches and fine leather of his boots were any indication. Of course, a brazen thief would steal all the riches he needed to live well. "Take my coin purse and go."

He frowned, his eyes turning to blue fire. "Madam, you insult me. I am no thief."

"Then why are you here?" Her head was spinning, and her heart was now painfully racing. She could not make it stop.

She clutched her chest.

Drat again!

She was going to pass out.

"Help me," she pleaded.

"Why should I?" His arms were still crossed over his chest, and he appeared to be making no move to lift a finger in assistance.

She fell to her knees. "You are a horrible man."

She heard him inhale sharply as her head hit the carpeted floor with a light thud. Perhaps it was her own intake of breath she'd heard as pain exploded across her brow, even though she had mostly managed to brace her fall.

"Bloody, foolish female," he muttered, kneeling beside her. "I thought you were faking."

Now her heart and her head felt as though they were about to burst. "I am not faking, you dolt." She refused to lose consciousness before she had told off this unspeakable bounder. "If I die, it will be all your fault...and..." She coughed from the strain of talking because it only made her body hurt worse. "I shall put a curse upon your soul...so that you shall never know a moment of..." She coughed again. "Not a moment of happiness from this day forth. I shall heap biblical plagues on you so that your skin will be covered in boils and—"

"Your lungs are quite healthy for someone who hit their head and seems about to pass out. Be quiet and lie still a moment," he said with surprising gentleness. "Save your breath about those curses. Someone has already heaped them on me."

Someone beat her to it?

What a disappointment.

She wasn't certain she believed him, for neither his body nor his face seemed the worse for wear. Up close, he was handsomer than she'd realized. Big and sturdy, and he smelled nice, too. Like something fruity and spicy and insanely appealing to her senses.

"Hen, what is your real name," he asked, his tone remaining surprisingly gentle.

But he still wasn't helping her up, and she was beginning to feel ridiculous lying with her cheek dug into the carpet and her body sprawled in a most unladylike fashion. Not that she cared at the moment, for her head was pounding like an ancient war drum, one of those enormous, deep monstrosities that took four soldiers and a cart to haul when advancing on the enemy.

After a moment, she struggled to sit up. However, she kept her eyes closed and put a hand to her brow. "Henleigh is my name. Lady Henleigh Killigrew."

He grunted. "An odd name for a female."

"But it is my name, whether you approve of it or not. What is yours?" She may as well know more about the man who was probably going to kill her after he had robbed her.

Yes, she ought to know his name, the better to properly curse him after she'd died.

"Captain Brioc Taran Arundel, at your service, Lady Henleigh."

"*Bree-ok*," she repeated softly. "And Arundel? Like the former owner of this cottage?" This explained why he marched across her property as though he owned it. He was probably related to the sea captain who had died here about a year ago. "Brioc is a Celtic name. What does it mean?"

Had he stayed on to tend the property when he was not sailing off to parts unknown himself?

This also explained his tanned body, for sailors would not feel the need to wear their shirts when toiling under the heat of the sun, especially outside of a lady's presence. But he ought to have known better than to keep it off now that she had come to reside here.

He cast her a wry smile. "Brioc means mighty, and Taran means thunder. Mighty thunder. Ironic since a storm of mighty thunder was the means of my undoing."

He knelt beside her, his skin so temptingly close she could almost kiss it. "Your undoing? What do you mean?"

"Have you not guessed who I am yet? Well, I suppose the lump on your head probably left you dazed and thinking slow."

"It has not!" The carpet was thick and soft enough to cushion much of her fall. She had hit her head, but the damage would have been worse had she not already fallen to her knees and braced her arms to absorb the worst of the impact.

"Is that so?" He arched a dark eyebrow. "Then who am I?"

She frowned at him. "Captain Brioc Taran Arundel. You've just told me."

"Who do you think I am to this property?"

She had no idea what he was talking about. "A relative of the deceased captain. I assume you look after this property whenever you return to Moonstone Landing from your sailings. You are a sea captain, too, are you not? I noticed it in the way you walk, a rather manly stride, but you plant your legs as though making your way across the deck of a ship as it rolls upon the waves."

He snorted. "And yet, you still have not made the connection."

"What connection? Obviously, you are related to the Captain Arundel who owned this cottage before me. I purchased it from his estate. Come to think of it, why did he not leave it to you? Did you have a falling out with him?"

"He and I are very close. As close as two people can possibly be. We think alike. We look alike. We even have the same name. We even have the same date of birth."

She glanced up at him. "But I thought he was an old man. That is…I just assumed he was."

He shook his head and sighed. "No, he died young. You don't get it, do you? We even have the same date of death." He stared at her. "And the same name. Really, Hen. How many more clues must I give you?"

She drew back with a start. "No!"

It could not be.

Her head began to spin again because it all suddenly made sense. "Are you the ghost?"

Chapter Two

"BRAVO, HEN," BRIOC said with a hearty chuckle. "I knew you would figure it out eventually."

Her beautiful eyes narrowed as she frowned at him. "I thought ghosts were supposed to be horrid and scary."

"Are you suggesting I am handsome?" He could not stop staring at this lovely creature who had taken over his bedchamber and stupidly run around the grounds of the cottage toting a rifle twice her size. He could tell she had never shot anything with it before by the amateurish way she had held it.

She blushed and began to stammer. "I am suggesting no such thing. Why I...of all the unspeakable arrogance. Put on your shirt and stop grinning at me. Since when do ghosts grin?"

No wonder her parents had given her the pet name Hen. This is what she was, a little clucking hen. But a lovely one.

Incredibly lovely, especially up close.

He would know, having had his share of women.

Her eyes were the color of dark chocolate, and her hair was a dark gold, full-bodied, and lush. Her bosom was also full and lush, as he had seen for himself the first night she had slept in his bedchamber. He had intended to scare her away, as he had done with all interlopers before her, but he made the mistake of arriving in time to watch her strip out of her gown and...well, any sane man would have kept his mouth shut and simply watched when coming upon such an exquisite sight.

He had settled in his favorite chair and studied her in fascination as she removed her corset with supple fingers, slipped off her chemise, and then slowly unpinned her hair and shook it loose so that those magnificent locks tumbled down her back in waves of gold silk.

She had gloriously full breasts, but the rest of her was rather slender.

All in all, he found her aspect quite delicate and pleasing despite her priggish nature. Yet, she also had a little of the firebrand in her, and he liked that.

What was she doing living alone in his cottage?

He asked her the question and was not surprised when she began to cluck at him again. But her voice was sweet and her body even sweeter, so he merely listened as she went on about women's rights and capabilities when a simple, one-sentence explanation would have sufficed.

"Really, Captain Arundel, you are too much. Why should I not own this cottage? Why should I not live by myself? What makes you think every woman is helpless and needs a man to handle matters for her?"

He merely arched an eyebrow, which she interpreted as another reason to take offense.

"Oh, and if you are so clever, then why do you haunt this cottage? You do realize that your presence here lowered its value. If it weren't for you, I would never have been able to purchase it as cheaply as I did." She tipped her head and cast him a smug smile. "So, there! Your rash actions allowed me to acquire this beautiful place for almost nothing. I think that makes me far shrewder in business affairs than you. And I'll have you know, I am quite adept at caring for myself. But with the money I've saved because you've scared the wits out of everyone from here to Falmouth, I can afford a staff to see to my daily comforts."

"Are you finished?"

She nodded.

"Good. You still haven't answered my question. Why are you living alone in my cottage?" He unfolded his arms and took a step toward her. "And kindly spare me the 'men are arses and woman are clever' lecture because my mother happened to be one of the smartest people I have ever met. If you knew anything about me—which you obviously do not, you would understand that I judge people on their merits, not their sex. Although, if I were not dead, I would surely be trying to have sex with you right now. So, answer my question. Why are you here alone?"

She attempted to slap his cheek, but her hand went through his face. "How dare you!"

He knew he should not have thrown in that last little bit about having sex with her, for she was a lady, and no one ought ever speak to her this way.

Nor would he have if he were still alive.

But he wasn't, and he found this most frustrating. She stirred something in him, a deep longing. No, stronger. Perhaps a craving. "Don't get your feathers in a ruffle, Hen."

She took a deep breath, filling her lungs, but he continued before she had the chance to let it out. "My point is, you are beautiful. You must have had at least a dozen men dropping to their knees to propose to you during your London season. How many seasons have you had? One? Two? You do not appear to be more than one and twenty years of age. Hardly twenty, if truth be told. Yet you must be old enough to acquire property on your own."

She released her breath in a soft exhale. "Oh, you think I am beautiful?"

He cast her a soft smile, surprised she did not realize just how exquisite she was. "Yes."

She blushed. "Thank you."

His expression softened. "I apologize if I was too brash with you. I am used to dealing with more…worldly women. I usually try to avoid virgins."

"Captain Arundel! Do you always say whatever pops into your head? Must you be so shockingly descriptive with your words?"

"Hen, if you are brave enough to live on your own…and I still have not received an answer to my question about it…then I think you have the mettle to withstand a little blunt speech. Or have I misread you? Are your sensibilities that delicate? Do you fall into a swoon at the slightest impropriety?"

She stared at her hands. "No. And why I am here is none of your business. I own the cottage now. I belong here. You do not."

He shook his head and sighed. "Now, that is where you are wrong. I am bound to this cottage far more strongly than you are. Need I remind you, I am dead. And yet, I have not moved on. Do you not wonder why? Most souls move on, do they not? So why haven't I?"

She began to nibble that sweet lower lip of hers. "That is actually an interesting question. Obviously, you've given it some thought. What do you think is the reason?"

He shrugged. "If I knew, I would do something about it."

She took a step closer, seeming to forget he had offended her with his blunt language only moments ago. She also seemed to forget she had just tried to slap him or that he still had not donned his shirt. "If you tell me what happened, perhaps I can help you figure it out."

Her eyes were that beautiful, dark color and looked quite extraordinary now, lit up like twinkling stars. "I'll think about it," he said, realizing he would quite enjoy haunting Hen. Well, not so much haunt her but appreciate her company.

His lack of enthusiasm to her suggestion must have surprised her, for her mouth gaped open. "You'll think about it?" She took a deep breath, ready to cluck at him again. "Oh, I see. You are happy to remain a misplaced soul, your spirit walking the earth, no one to see you, touch you…care about you."

"You can see me."

She cleared her throat. "You are missing my point. Why do you wish to be chained to this cottage for eternity? Does it not pain you to watch time march on, to see your loved ones die and move on, yet you remain stuck here?"

"I only died a year ago, to be precise."

Hen sank back in the plump chair by the hearth, his favorite chair with a matching ottoman that allowed him to put up his feet and relax as he sat by the fire, a book in one hand and a brandy in the other.

He had purchased the chair and ottoman in Constantinople on one of his seafaring journeys. The cottage was filled with things he had picked up in his travels around the world. Apparently, his solicitor had not bothered packing them up or selling them off, just dumped the problem of disposing of them on Hen.

In truth, he did not mind that his house had been left as a sort of shrine to him. Besides, it was quite comfortable returning night after night to a familiar spot.

"How did you die, Captain Arundel?"

Since she was now in the chair with her feet curled under her bottom, that left the ottoman free for him. He sat down on it and looked at her. "I drowned at sea. In a storm, as I mentioned earlier."

"Yes, how tragic. I am truly sorry." She reached out to touch his arm, then realized it would only slip through the air and drew it away.

"Thank you, Hen." He nodded to acknowledge her words. "Do you mind if I put on my shirt?"

She laughed and shook her head. "Am I hearing right? You intend to behave like a gentleman now?"

He regarded her wryly. "I needn't if you are opposed to—"

"Please do! It is quite unsettling to entertain a bare-chested man in my bedchamber. I did not expect you to volunteer to properly dress yourself."

"It is *our* bedchamber," he said, liking the soft blush that crept up her cheeks at his words. "And just to be clear, you never need dress on my account. I will never demand it of you."

She attempted to swat his shoulder, but her hand simply pushed through him. "Why did I think you had turned into a gentleman?"

He threw his head back and laughed. "Oh, Hen. I am certainly no gentleman. Do not ever mistake me for one."

He slapped his hands on his thighs and rose. "Well, I hear your staff arriving. It is time I left."

He started for the balcony.

"Captain Arundel, wait." She followed him to the double doors that opened onto the balcony. "Must you go? You've told me so little of yourself or this puzzle we must sort out about your haunting this cottage."

He stared down at her, wanting to kiss her soft lips. "I'll frighten your staff, and then you will have no one to look after you. I'll return when they've gone."

"Please do." She began to wring her hands.

"Hen? Why are you fretting?"

"I am afraid if I let you go, you will never come back."

Pain filled him.

He wanted to cup her face and kiss her sweetly.

When had anyone ever cared whether he lived or died? Indeed, with his parents gone years before him, his closest relations were distant cousins who had wanted nothing to do with him in life and even less so now that he was dead.

Of course, he understood Hen's interest in him had more to do with her love of puzzles. He doubted she cared for him beyond figuring out why he was still here.

Yet, he detected warmth and sincere concern in her eyes.

Why had no one snapped up this beautiful girl during her first season out?

"I am bound here, Hen. I will always come back to you. But I have a question for you." He ached to touch her and silently cursed his fate that he could not. "Why do you care?"

Chapter Three

A S SOON AS Captain Arundel had disappeared, Henleigh washed and dressed, then hurried downstairs and kept herself busy into the late morning supervising chores around the house. There was not much to do since only she occupied the house and tended to tidy up after herself as a matter of course.

"I've finished, Lady Henleigh. Is there anything else ye'd like me to do before I leave?" Marjorie, her young maid, asked before walking back to the village of Moonstone Landing, where she lived with her parents and six siblings.

The day was sparkling, one of those fine summer days when the sun shone brightly and the light breeze off the water kept the heat manageable. "Wait a moment, Marjorie. I'll fetch my bonnet and walk into the village with you."

She hurried into the kitchen to speak to the couple she had hired as cook and groundskeeper. The husband had just finished pulling up a patch of weeds by the cliff steps and repairing a few of those steps that had come loose. His wife was just removing a pot off the hearth.

"Is that lamb stew, Mrs. Hawke?" she asked, already knowing the answer, for the delicious aroma was unmistakable.

Mrs. Hawke set the pot down with a *thunk* onto the sturdy work-table. "Yes, m'lady. It is."

"Oh, thank you. My stomach is growling already." She cast her a warm smile. "I've decided to walk into town. You and your husband may leave whenever you've finished today's chores. Are there any supplies I should order while I am wandering about?"

"No, m'lady," the friendly woman replied, her cheeks apple-red from standing close to the hearth fire. "I have all I need."

Mr. Hawke said much the same. "I'll let ye know if I think of anything, m'lady. But there's nothing for this week."

"Very well." She waved to them as she hurried off with Marjorie.

She and her maid, who seemed a little uncomfortable walking with her, parted ways as soon as they reached town.

Henleigh realized she might have been too friendly with Marjorie. The girl was not used to conversing with someone of her social standing. Perhaps this would change over time.

As much of it as I have left.

Who could ever know when their time was up?

She shrugged off the thought and went to pay a call on the Moonstone Landing agent who had sold her Captain Arundel's property. "Mr. Priam, may I have a moment of your time?"

He eyed her warily. "I cannot undo the sale. I warned you about the ghost. I was quite up front with it, and you knew what you were purchasing."

"I did not come for this reason," she said with marked impatience. "I have no quarrel with the ghost."

"You don't?" He appeared surprised, which meant Captain Arundel usually wasted no time in scaring off visitors to his property. "Please have a seat, Lady Henleigh. Why have you come to see me then?"

"I am here because I wish to know more about my ghost, especially how he died." She cleared her throat. "You see, I am a bit of a historian, and I thought it would be an interesting project for me to undertake."

"Ah, then it is the schoolmistress you must ask, for she was there with her class when the unfortunate incident occurred. The school-house is just down the street. Miss Gray usually allows the children outside for a few minutes to run around and have their lunch about now. I would escort you, but I have clients waiting for me, and I am late already. You cannot miss the schoolhouse or Miss Gray. She is a young woman, perhaps a few years older than you. A pretty brunette with a happy countenance."

"The schoolmistress?" She tried not to sound dismayed, although why should she care if Captain Arundel was sweet on the woman? It was none of her concern at all.

Henleigh rose. "Then I shall be on my way."

She hurried down the road, quickening her pace when she saw the children already playing outside. "Miss Gray, may I have a word with you?" she asked, easily recognizing the young woman in charge. She was as Mr. Priam had described, dark hair and a lovely smile. He had neglected to mention the emerald sparkle of her eyes. "I am Lady Henleigh Killigrew, and I have just purchased Moonstone Cottage."

Had Captain Arundel been in love with her?

"Oh, yes. The village is all astir about you. The local bookmaker is taking odds on how long you will last before hurrying back to London and putting the cottage up for sale." She shook her head. "It is shameful. The captain was a very good man and deserves better than to be the object of such a wager."

A knot of dismay curled in Henleigh's belly. "You knew him well, it seems."

"No, not at all, really. We had never met until he saved my life and those of the children." She motioned for Henleigh to join her in the shade of a nearby oak tree.

Henleigh blushed.

Had she built up a romance for him in her mind?

Perhaps he had loved Miss Gray from afar and never had the courage to step forward. She silently laughed at the thought. The captain was the sort who went after what he wanted and would let nothing stand in his way.

"This is why I am here," she said, clearing her head of all other thoughts. "I am an amateur historian and would like to do something at the cottage to commemorate his life. You say he saved you and the children? What happened?"

"There was a fair going on in the village, amusements set up in the village green all week long and boat rides offered. The day was particularly fine, so I took the class down to the dock, and we all got on one of the sloops offering a ride around the harbor. There was no charge for us because…well, I am now betrothed to the young man who owns the vessel."

"Oh, how lovely. Congratulations. Have you set a wedding date?"

She nodded shyly. "Yes, we are to be married next month. We owe our joy to Captain Arundel. None of us would be here were it not for his bravery. But as I was saying, the day was lovely, so we were quite unprepared when hit by a sudden squall."

"A squall?"

"Yes, one of those once-in-a-decade violent storms that blows in with torrential force and is gone within twenty minutes, but not before it wreaks havoc upon all in its path. Our sloop was battered and buffeted amid all the thunder and fury, then shoved onto the rocks, damaging the hull so badly, we began to sink."

Henleigh put a hand to her throat. "Oh, my!"

"The storm had yet to move off, but Captain Arundel did not spare a moment in coming to our rescue. He kept a sailboat in the harbor that I am told he loved to take out at sunset. He ran to it, jumped in with a few other men, and sailed out to rescue us. I was amazed his boat did not capsize, for the waves were high, and the water was a dangerous swirl that formed riptides and whirlpools everywhere. But he was an expert sailor and knew how to handle the wind and the water."

"Then what happened?"

"The squall had almost passed by the time he reached us, so he was able to maneuver his vessel close to ours and start hauling the children off it. He got them all onto his. Me, as well. Then he sailed to the nearest beach where other rescuers were standing in wait to unload us. Then he went back for the crew."

Henleigh took out her handkerchief as Miss Gray spoke, for the young woman's story and her quiet tears also brought tears to her eyes. "How many were you all together?"

"Ten children, me, and a crew of six. The wind was still howling, and we could hear the sharp crack of wood as the sloop began to break apart. Captain Arundel did not waver. He was helping my Henry get one of his injured men onto his sailboat when the sloop's giant mast suddenly cracked and hit him on the head, knocking him into the sea."

Tears streamed down Henleigh's cheeks. "And they could not save him?"

Miss Gray shook her head. "They tried desperately, but it was as though the sea had reached up its mighty jaws and swallowed him. They never saw him surface, not even once in all the hours spent searching after the squall had passed. We were all devastated by his loss. We never recovered his body. It must have been swept out into the English Channel by those dangerous tides and wave swells."

Henleigh's heart ached for him. "I suppose it is fitting the sea took him."

Miss Gray nodded. "He truly loved the sea. I am told that he only came back to land in order to arrange his next sailing."

"I must do something to honor his memory." She dabbed her eyes and cheeks. "I had no idea he was someone quite so special."

"He is a hero to us all. I had never met him before that day. Suddenly, he was before us, shouting orders and calming all of us, assuring us we would all survive. He was our guardian angel that day."

The schoolboys were starting to get unruly.

Miss Gray turned in dismay as two of the boys began to scuffle. "Lady Henleigh, do forgive me. I must get the children back inside."

"I won't delay you. Thank you for your time, Miss Gray. I shall invite you up to the cottage for tea once I am settled in."

"I would love that," she said and hurried off.

Henleigh walked down to the dock and stared out across the quiet harbor. The sun glistened on the water, reflecting off it like sparkling diamonds. The wind had picked up, so that whitecaps now formed on the heightening waves. She thought she saw a family of dolphins in the distance but could not be sure.

Sailboats and a few fishing boats were moored near the dock, their ropes groaning as they were pulled taut with the ebb and flow of the tide. Other vessels were out on the water, dotting the harbor, some cutting across it with neatly trimmed sails caught on the breeze.

She inhaled the scent of salt air and fish and weathered wood. "I wish I could hug you, Captain Arundel," she murmured. "It is beautiful here. I can see why you loved it."

"I'm glad you like Moonstone Landing, Hen."

She turned sharply to the deep rumble of his voice and saw him come to stand beside her. He was still clad in the same clothes he had worn this morning, his shirt thankfully still on and now neatly tucked into his breeches.

Truly, he was a fine-looking man.

She shook her head in confusion. "Captain? How can you be here?"

She glanced around, hoping no one caught her talking to him. They must already think her mad to have settled at his cottage. To now be seen talking to herself would raise more eyebrows.

"Should I not be?"

She glanced around once more and put a gloved hand to her mouth, pretending to cough as she spoke to him. "I thought you were bound to the cottage?"

"I am, but that does not mean I cannot go anywhere else. Moonstone Landing is a charming town, do you not think so, Hen?"

She faked another cough. "Yes."

He laughed. "Ah, you are afraid people will see you talking to yourself and start calling you the Mad Woman of Moonstone Cottage. We shall save our chat until later this evening. But I would like to escort you around town and point out the sights. Do you mind?"

"Not at all. Just don't expect me to talk to you."

"You needn't. I rather like the idea of walking beside you in companionable silence." He looked around. "I haven't been down here in a while. Very little has changed."

They left the dock and returned to the center of town, passing a row of fishmongers and their wagons, and several taverns close to the dock. Further up the street were several farm stands selling fresh produce, a butcher's shop, bakery, fabrics shop, tea shop, the land agent's office, a solicitor's office, the blacksmith's stable, a carpenter's workplace, and an inn.

Grazing sheep dotted the village green, and several tinkers had gaily festooned wagons parked along one side of it displaying crockery, trinkets and ribbons, and other wares.

"Wednesday is market day in Moonstone Landing. The green will be packed with stands and wagons then. You'll be able to find almost anything you need." He turned to study her. "You look tired, Hen. I think Miss Gray's story took much out of you."

She smiled at him. "I do not think I can ever hate you after learning what you did. Please accept my apology for any rudeness I may have displayed toward you."

"No apology needed," he said with a rakish grin. "I am still an arrogant arse, even if I do have a few redeeming qualities. But come on, you do look pale. I'll walk you to the tea shop. Mrs. Halsey makes the best cherry pie. She also has an excellent mint tea."

The sky had grown overcast, so she hurried to Mrs. Halsey's shop and sat at one of the tables. She ordered the cherry pie and mint tea and ate as the rain began to fall in earnest.

Captain Arundel was still regarding her with concern. "The rain will pass soon. It always does. But the roadway will be muddy. Mrs. Halsey's husband keeps a cart out back. He'll take you back home. You shouldn't walk, Hen."

She gave him a subtle nod and then polished off her slice of pie.

The rain had stopped by the time she drank the last of her tea. "That was delicious, Mrs. Halsey. I think I shall take an entire one home with me."

The portly woman laughed. "Cherry pie was the captain's favorite, too."

Henleigh nodded. "Then I shall leave a slice out for him."

The woman glanced around, then whispered. "Have you seen him yet, my lady? Cherry pie and mint tea was what he ordered whenever he came into my shop."

Henleigh tried not to blush, but she was never very good at hiding her feelings. Instead, she tried to make a jest of it. "Perhaps he came to me in my sleep and whispered in my ear about your pie and tea. I shall have to thank him, for the recommendation was excellent. I shall bring my nieces around first thing when they come to visit."

Mrs. Halsey tittered. "I look forward to it."

Henleigh rose to peer out the window. "May I trouble your husband for a ride home?"

"No trouble at all, m'lady." She bustled into the kitchen, calling for Mr. Halsey.

The tea shop had emptied out now that the rain stopped.

She and the captain were alone for the moment.

"Hen," he said gently, "you have nieces?"

She nodded. "Three lovely little girls. My brother's daughters."

He frowned. "Would your brother not permit you to live with him? Or was it his wife who chased you away?"

"Neither of them. In truth, they wanted me to stay with them and were very disappointed when I purchased your cottage. They'll come to visit me soon, and you will meet them. But you mustn't scare any of them, or I shall never forgive you."

"Heap more curses on my soul?" He laughed softly but soon turned serious. "I wouldn't harm your family. They seem very nice."

"They are. My brother is a very kind man. We have always been close. He married a lovely young woman, who thinks of me as a sister. I am godmother to their eldest girl. She has my name, but hers is spelled H-e-n-l-e-y. I plan to leave the cottage to her upon my—" She gave a ridiculous giggle. "Well, I am getting ahead of myself, aren't I?"

The captain remained serious in his regard. "Are you?"

"Why are you staring at me like that?"

His gaze bore into her as though he were trying to reach into her soul. "Why are you here, Hen? What is really going on with you?"

Chapter Four

A S SOON AS the sun had set and Hen had retired to his bedchamber, Brioc put in his appearance. He had arrived earlier but said nothing while she undressed and readied herself for bed, going through the same routine he had watched her go through each night. First, slipping out of her gown, then untying the laces of her corset, and finally removing her chemise to reveal her exquisite body.

She quickly washed the day's dirt off herself with lavender soap and afterward donned the serviceable nightrail she had set out for herself on the bed.

His bed.

She belonged in it.

If only he could lie beside her and wrap her in his arms.

Were he still alive, he might have done something about getting her into his bed and keeping her beside him always.

Yes, he might have married a girl like Hen.

He watched her toss her robe over her thin, white nightgown before sitting down in the chair beside the hearth. She had a brush in her hand and began to brush her magnificent curls.

These summer nights were too warm for a fire, so she had lit the lamp on his desk to provide the room with illumination. It now cast a warm, amber glow about his bedchamber.

He could stare at her all night like this, her face soft and glowing in the gentle light.

Not wanting to startle her, he waited for her to look around the room for him and call out his name before he showed himself. "I was wondering where you were," she said as he strode toward her and took his usual seat beside her on the ottoman.

"I want answers, Hen."

She set aside her brush and frowned at him. "What do you mean?"

"How many times must I ask the question before I get a straight answer out of you? Why are you here?"

"Why should I not be here?"

"Don't give me that indignant look. I will not be put off this time." He leaned toward her, wishing he could take hold of her hands. "You have a brother who loves you. A sister-in-law who thinks of you as a sister. Nieces you obviously adore. Do they live in London?"

She nodded.

"Yet, you have left them to come all this way across the south of England to Moonstone Landing and settle here, *alone*, in my cottage. Cornwall is an awfully long way from London. Why, Hen?"

"I do not wish to talk about it."

"I am a ghost. I shall haunt you until you do. So you may as well spare yourself the ordeal and talk to me. Is there a scandal attached to you?"

She snorted. "No."

He believed her.

She obviously knew nothing about men.

He loved that innocence about her.

"Why will you not believe that I fell in love with this cottage and wanted it for my own? It is beautiful here, a paradise on earth. I can see why you loved it, too. The formal rooms are elegant but not too large. The bedchambers are beautifully appointed. Yours has a stunning view of the garden and sea. The town of Moonstone Landing is charming. The sea air is bracing. The weather is warm and inviting.

Why should I not want to be here?"

"You are still dissembling, Hen. Why will you not trust me with the truth? I will find out eventually, just as you are determined to find out the reason why I am still bound here even though I am dead."

She had been clutching her robe as they spoke, but he suddenly realized that it was her heart she was clutching. She did that a lot. Perhaps it was just a mannerism. He supposed genteel, young ladies often clutched their hearts when faced with indelicate matters.

But this wasn't Hen.

Yes, she was sweet and delicate in some ways. But she was not frail in spirit. It frustrated him not to understand what was going on with her. "Perhaps I ought to pay a call on your brother and learn the truth from him."

She cast him a doubtful look. "Ha! How can you?"

He folded his arms across his chest. "Ghosts can travel wherever they like."

She pursed her lips. "Is this some ghostly lore? I don't believe you. I think you are making it up."

"As you wish. Care to call my bluff? I can be in London visiting your brother within the hour. That's another advantage to being a ghost. We can travel faster than you."

She sighed in dismay. "No, don't go. Why can you not leave me and my circumstances alone? I came here to avoid having to answer to anyone or face their pitying looks."

His eyes widened in surprise. "Why would they give you pitying looks?"

Hen was beautiful, smart, and not in want of funds. Probably not in want of suitors either. She had it all, did she not? "Are you in mourning for someone you loved?"

Yet, she did not dress in mourning attire. Nor had he noticed any miniature portrait or other token of a man's love either carried in a locket or pinned to her gown.

She rose and walked over to his bureau. "I found this today while looking through your things." She held up a painted miniature portrait of himself. "It is a very good likeness. It must have been done shortly before your...you know."

"My death? Yes, it was." He folded his arms across his chest and cast her a rakish smile. "It was done on my last trip to France. I was in Honfleur picking up lace, perfumes, and wine to bring back to England. While strolling near their docks, I met an artist who offered to paint my portrait."

Hen took another moment to study it, turning the miniature over in her soft hands. "He is obviously talented. He did a very nice job."

"She."

"What?"

"The artist was a woman. Married to a wealthy count who did not seem to mind her...er, free-spirited nature. The French are that way, unlike the pinch-lipped English, who are all about setting rules on what others should do."

Hen dropped the miniature in his top drawer and shut it with a slam. "I ought to have realized. Have you no shame?"

"Me? I was not the married one. If it did not bother her or her husband, where is the harm? I got a lovely portrait out of it. Kindly do not throw it away. It might be worth something someday. She did have artistic talent."

"Among other talents," Hen muttered, sounding quite indignant...or was that jealousy he was noting?

"I am not suggesting I would ever break my marriage vows," he said, although he did not see that he owed Hen any explanation. "I am simply not condemning others who do. It is none of my business what consenting adults decide to do."

Those warm, chocolate eyes of hers sought his own. "Oh, really? You would be faithful to your wife?"

He reached out and ran his knuckle along the line of her jaw, knowing he could not feel the softness of her skin. Nor could she feel his hand. Still, he needed to caress her. "If you were my wife, I would love you always. I would never break my vows to you."

She eyed him with pain. "I am tired, Captain Arundel. I think I must go to sleep."

He nodded. "Will you at least call me Brioc? The formality seems unnecessary since you sleep each night in my bed."

"I sleep there, but I don't *sleep* there...not with you."

He arched an eyebrow.

She sighed. "I do not want to know if you sleep there, too. All right? Keep it to yourself. We cannot touch each other or feel each other anyway, so it does not count."

"Fine, I will not mention it. Are you angry with me, Hen?"

"No, how can I ever be? Good night, Brioc. Thank you for showing me around the village today. I really enjoyed myself. And..."

"What is it, Hen?"

"Thank you for rescuing Miss Gray and her students. That was such a brave and magnificently noble thing you did."

He shrugged. "Others sailed out to the sinking sloop with me."

"But you led the way. No one else could have done what you did. I'm sorry I snapped at you. I wish I could touch you," she said in a shaky whisper and closed her eyes. "I am so proud of you and so honored you have allowed me to move into your cottage. I will treasure it and the memory of you forever."

He leaned forward and put his lips to hers, knowing neither of them could feel the kiss. But he needed to kiss her just the same.

He imagined the taste of cherry pie and mint tea on her tongue.

"Sweet dreams, my lovely Hen."

She opened her eyes and stared at him in confusion. "What's wrong?" he asked.

"You kissed me."

He nodded. "I appreciated your words. Do you mind? I know you could not feel my lips on yours, but the gesture was important to me."

She shook her head. "No, you don't understand. You kissed me...and I felt it."

Was she jesting?

She did not appear to be.

Her eyes were wide as full moons, and her fingers were lightly pressed to her soft lips. "Hen, it cannot be."

"Try it again."

"With pleasure," he murmured and bent his head to hers as she tipped hers up to him. He pressed his mouth over hers. A flood of warmth tore through him, but he did not feel her mouth against his, could only imagine the soft give of her lips.

He drew away and began to trail kisses down her neck, inhaling the scent of lavender on her skin. "Can you feel this, Hen?"

"Oh...my...yes."

He drew back, feeling bloody-well confused.

Her cheeks were a bright pink, and her eyes held a look quite familiar to him, that of a woman aroused. But it was completely unfamiliar to Hen. She did not understand what her body needed, wanted, or that it was missing something only he could provide. "Now we have another puzzle to solve," she said in a breathless whisper. "Why can I feel your kisses?"

He had no answer for her.

Nor did he know why he was still bound to the cottage.

Or why Hen was here on her own, forsaking her obviously loving family.

Perhaps tomorrow would bring answers.

In any event, the hour was growing late, and Hen looked tired. "Come to bed," he said, holding out his hand.

She regarded him quizzically, then nodded and reached for it.

To both their disappointment, her hand simply slid through his outstretched fingers. "Did you feel anything, Hen?"

"No. I'm so sorry. I wanted to."

"It's all right."

She crossed to the bed and removed her robe, then scampered under the covers. She lay back contentedly and turned on her side to watch him. "Where do you sleep, Brioc? Or do ghosts never sleep?"

He had jested earlier about sleeping by her side, but he could not remember where he slept or if he ever did.

All he recalled was swimming along the beach each morning at dawn and then climbing the stairs to his cottage. It had been his routine when he was alive and residing in Moonstone Landing between hauling merchandise to different parts of the world and back.

He made up a story for Hen, knowing it would upset her to know the hollowness of his existence. "I stretch out on the chair beside the hearth, my legs across the ottoman. On warm nights, I'll sleep on the balcony under a blanket of stars."

"That sounds lovely."

"Have you ever tried it, Hen? Sleeping outdoors, the gentle breeze to cool you, and a thousand stars to light up the night sky."

"No, never. It sounds wonderful. May we try it one night?" She yawned. "But not tonight. I am suddenly so tired. Do you mind if we put it off for another time?"

"I don't mind, Hen." He leaned over and kissed her on the forehead as she closed her eyes. She did not respond to his touch this time, so he expected she had not felt it.

He swallowed his disappointment.

"Sweet dreams, Hen."

"You too, Brioc. I shall keep you in my dreams tonight."

She was curled up on one side of his big bed, so he stretched out beside her. Their bodies did not touch, nor did he attempt to reach for her.

He just needed to be near her.

He, too, closed his eyes and fell asleep amid thinking up answers to his questions.

Why was he still here?

Why had Hen come here?

How could she possibly feel his kisses?

Could the answers to these questions be connected?

Chapter Five

HENLEIGH AWOKE AT dawn to stand on the balcony of her bedchamber. She peered into the mist, eager for the sight of Brioc making his way up the cliff stairs and crossing her garden, his shirt casually slung over his shoulder.

She was no longer offended by his appearance.

In truth, after feeling his kisses last night, she ached to feel more of him. Would his skin be warm against her palms? What would those splendid muscles of his feel like as she ran her hands over them? And the spray of dark curls across his chest? Would the hair be springy or soft?

She shook her head and sighed.

How easily he had turned her into a wanton.

Then she saw him through the disappearing mist, his arms and chest glistening from the drops of water he had not bothered to dry off after donning his boots and breeches. His shirt was slung over one shoulder, as usual. "Brioc," she called out to him softly.

He glanced up and smiled at her. "Good morning, Hen."

She let out a breath of relief and smiled back. "Did you sleep well?"

He laughed. "Yes. How about you?"

She nodded. "Quite well, thank you. Come around to the front of the house. I'll unlatch the door to let you in."

"You needn't. A latched door won't keep me out. I'll be up in a moment."

She used her fingers to brush back a few stray wisps of her braided hair and adjusted the belt of her robe. Most of her robes were loose, stiff, and buttoned down the front, but this one was of softest cotton and merely had a belt to wrap around her waist instead of all those buttons. She liked the way it clung to her body and hoped Brioc would find it attractive as well.

"Don't you look pretty this morning, Hen," he said, suddenly in her bedchamber and striding across it to join her on the balcony.

She smiled shyly. "Thank you. I expect I am a mess, but you are too polite to say otherwise."

He had donned his shirt and had it neatly tucked in the waistband of his breeches once again. She swallowed her disappointment.

Those big muscles of his, attached to his hard, lean body, were beckoning for her exploration.

"What do you have planned today?" he asked, regaining her attention while she very discreetly ogled his body.

"Nothing in particular," she said casually, hoping he had not noticed. "If the morning turns out nice, I thought I might take a walk along the beach."

"I like the idea. It will be a nice day. I can tell by how quickly the mist is burning off the water. It will be rather hot, which should keep the water calm. Have Mrs. Hawke pack you a picnic lunch. Bring along a blanket to stretch out on and a bonnet to protect your face while you bask in the sun."

"All right." She returned indoors and was about to ask him to give her a few minutes of privacy, but he had disappeared. She hurried onto the balcony again and saw him standing by the cliff stairs, staring down at the water.

Within the hour, Marjorie and the Hawkes had arrived.

She had washed, dressed, and done up her hair, eager to get down to the beach. She asked Mrs. Hawke to pack her a basket and Marjorie to give her an old blanket to set out on the sand. Then she was off to meet Brioc, excited what this new day would bring.

There were more steps than she realized.

They were steep, too.

She carefully made her way down.

Climbing them would be much harder, but she would take her time and rest as she needed. Perhaps there was an easier path back to the cottage. Brioc would know and show her.

Her shoes sank into the soft sand the moment she stepped onto the beach.

She paused to take in the view.

The sand was a buttery yellow in contrast to the red of the cliff stone.

The water was the deepest blue.

The breeze was light and salty as it brushed her cheeks.

"Brioc, are you here?" She set out her blanket and picnic basket, tossed off her bonnet, shoes, and stockings, and then lifted her gown to her knees so that she could dip her feet in the water.

"It's cold!" She gasped but held firm and walked in up to her ankles, giggling as the waves rushed in and tickled her legs as they drew back.

"It's nice, isn't it?" Brioc said, coming up behind her.

"It is glorious." She cast him a brilliant smile. "This is a wonderful idea. I have never done this before."

"Can you swim?"

"No."

"Ah, be careful then. Do not go in beyond your knees. The tug of the water is powerful."

"I won't." She regarded him thoughtfully.

His eyes held amusement as he returned her gaze. "What are you thinking, Hen?"

"They never found your body. Do you know where it is? If I find it, I can give you a proper burial. Perhaps this is why you are still bound here."

"No, that is not the reason. Nothing to do with my body. It is just flesh and bone. Besides, it will never be found. It washed out into the English Channel and carried to the ocean beyond to be eaten by sharks. Hen, do not look so distraught. I was long dead. I did not feel a thing."

Tears welled in her eyes. "I cannot help aching for you. What happened to you is so unfair."

He shrugged. "That is life, isn't it? Often tragic and unfair. But I love the sea. I did not mind dying there."

"If you do not think it is your unrecovered body interfering with your release from the cottage, then what do you think is the reason?" She hastily raised her gown to her thighs as a strong wave suddenly surrounded her, and water surged above her knees.

The surge of water tugged at her as it ebbed, drawing her a few steps deeper. She managed to break away from its strong pull and darted back onto land.

"Careful, Hen. I told you, the water is powerful."

She nodded. "I see. And you say it is calm today? How ever were you able to reach the sloop with the storm raging? What you did in saving the schoolteacher and her pupils is nothing short of a miracle."

He cast her a wry grin. "I may be a cad, but I do have some redeeming qualities. I could not let those children drown."

She pursed her lips in thought. "Perhaps you are here as a reward for your good deed. Do you think it is possible? That the angels left you here because this is the place you love."

"No, Hen. As beautiful as it is and as much as I did love Moonstone Cottage, I do not have an unbreakable attachment to it or the village. Come, let's walk along the beach. Keep to the water's edge."

"All right." She liked walking beside him. There was something lovely about being beside this man, her toes sinking into the wet sand

and the sun shining down upon her head. Kittiwakes and kestrels hovered over the water in search of fish, then flew back to their nests amid the carved-out rocks upon the cliff face.

The breeze was stronger down here and blew through her hair. She had left it loose but tied back at her nape by a simple ribbon—a green ribbon to match the green flowers embroidered on her gown of white muslin.

"You look pretty, Hen."

She blushed. "Thank you."

He smiled rakishly. "You are not used to gentlemen giving you compliments."

"I spent two seasons as a wallflower."

He stopped and looked at her askance, ignoring the breeze as it blew through his dark hair, and the water as it rushed to lap the soles of his boots. "Impossible. You are a diamond of the first water."

She shook her head. "I looked like a frightened doe most of the time. My gowns were out of style, and I did not dance well at all. Nor did I much like the gentlemen who approached me. Oh, there were plenty of them at first. But they quickly disappeared when they learned I was not an heiress. It suited me just fine."

His expression darkened. "Was there not a decent man among them?"

She pursed her lips. "Perhaps, but I was not confident enough of myself to tell the decent ones from the scoundrels, so I chased them all away."

"Would you have chased me away, I wonder?"

"Yes, I fear so. You would have frightened me most of all. Some-one as handsome as you? I would have been a stammering ninny."

"I like to think I would have seen beyond your shyness and tried to put you at ease."

She continued to walk along the beach, her gown now only hiked to her calves. She supposed it was still scandalous, but she doubted

Brioc would complain. He seemed the sort to appreciate a woman's legs. "I don't know. There were so many pretty young ladies having their come-outs at the same time as I was. I don't think you would have bothered with me."

"I suppose it is a moot point now. I am dead, and we shall never know what might have happened between us had we ever met."

She picked up a shell and cleaned it off in the water. "This one's quite pretty. Look how it shines inside. Like a pink pearl. Or an opal, perhaps."

"That iridescent shine is called nacre."

"Well, look at that. It is beautiful. Thank you for teaching me something new."

"You are most welcome. Are you hungry, Hen? We ought to head back to the blanket now."

"All right." She wiggled her toes in the warm sand a moment before heading back the way they came. "The waves are lapping the shore with more force now."

"The tide is coming in. Don't worry, it will not reach your blanket. I would have warned you if you'd spread it too close to the water. But step back a little as we walk, or those rogue waves will knock you over."

"I think I would have liked you had I met you earlier, Brioc. Of course, I would have been too shy ever to approach you. I would have swooned if you had ever approached me."

He grinned. "I would have swooned over you, too."

She shook her head and laughed heartily. "I doubt it. Our meeting would never have come to anything. As I said, I was a tongue-tied nitwit and just wanted to lose myself against the wall most of the time."

They returned to the blanket, and she took out the bread and cheese Mrs. Hawke had packed for her. She had also packed a bottle of lemonade and put a cork in it as one would for wine. She struggled to pull it out. "Ugh, it's tightly stuck in there."

"Sorry, Hen. I would help if I could."

"I know." She gave a final pull, smacking her fisted hand against her chest as she drew it out. "Ow," she cried, dropping the bottle to clasp her heart.

Of all the stupid things to do.

Brioc was on his knees beside her in a trice. "Hen? What's wrong? Did you hurt yourself?"

She nodded. "I'll be all right in a moment."

He remained beside her, worry filling his eyes. "You hit your heart," he said, almost to himself.

She ignored the comment.

She had come here to avoid just this discussion with her brother. She refused to have it now with Brioc.

She straightened the bottle, ignoring the fact that most of the lemonade had spilled onto the sand. After wiping off the bits of sand, she took a swig and then replaced the cork. "I just need to lie back a moment and close my eyes."

He took her hand as she lay back.

How could she feel his kisses last night and now his big, warm hand wrapping around hers? She dared not say anything, for this ability seemed to go only one way. She felt his touch, but he did not feel hers.

She sat up a few minutes later and tore off the end of the loaf of bread. She nibbled a little of the cheese, as well, needing little more than a few bites to satisfy her hunger.

Brioc stared at her. "You eat like a mouse."

"I wasn't very hungry."

"Because of your heart?"

"There is nothing wrong with my heart."

He stretched out on the blanket. "Fine, Hen. Keep lying to me."

"I think I had better return to the cottage. Would you mind getting your oafish body off my blanket so I can fold it up?"

"Go ahead. No one's stopping you. I am nothing but air. You can easily pull it out from under me. Last night I was your hero. Now I am an oaf?"

She sighed and glanced up the flight of stairs leading back to the cottage. "No. You shall always be my hero. But right now, you are irritating me." She would never make it up those steps without having to stop and rest. Then Brioc would be asking more questions. "Is there an easy walk further along the beach where the climb is not so steep?"

"No, Hen. Well, there is. But it adds about five miles, and I do not think you can walk that distance. The stairs are the simplest. Take your time. I'll be right beside you all the while. Take as long as your heart needs. Why hide the truth from me?"

She covered her face with her hands and began to cry. "I did not want anyone to know."

"You cannot hide it from those close to you, Hen. Does your brother know?"

"Yes, unfortunately."

"It all makes sense now. You did not care about a ghost haunting this cottage because you came out here to die." She felt his arm go around her shoulders to comfort her. Why was she now able to feel him? "I wish you had confided in me. Of all people, I think I would be the one to understand best."

"I don't want to talk about it. Please don't make me."

He grunted. "I won't. But I do want to hear all of it when you are ready. In your own good time. I won't press you."

He sat by her side until she stopped crying and then rose along with her when she gathered the blanket and picnic basket. She had tossed her bonnet, shoes, and stockings in the blanket and began to climb the steps in her bare feet.

She climbed the first twenty steps, then stopped to rest, waiting for her heart to stop pounding through her chest before she started to climb again. She made it up the next twenty steps and rested again.

Brioc watched her.

She was about to climb the next twenty when someone at the top called out her name. "Hen, are you mad? You know what the doctor said!"

"Who is that?" Brioc asked.

"My brother." She waited for Robert to descend to her, his attire the height of London fashion, and his golden hair ruffled by the wind. She hugged him fiercely when he took her in his arms to embrace her. "Robert, what are you doing here?"

She did not object when he took the basket and blanket out of her hands. "I've come to take you back home."

"No," she said, stiffening. "I am home. Moonstone Cottage is my home now."

"Nonsense, Hen. You belong with us. I've brought Anne and the girls with me to convince you. Henley, Phoebe, and Chloe missed you desperately and cannot wait to see you again."

She groaned. "You shouldn't have done that. I won't go with you, and now the girls will be heartbroken all over again. Stay the week, but then you must go home."

"Hen," he said with a wrenching groan, "you are my little sister. How can I abandon you?"

She glanced over his shoulder to Brioc, who was right behind him and taking in every word. "You are not abandoning me. I am happy here. Truly. I will show you. The girls will have so much fun here. I'll take them down to the dock and show them the fish market. Then we can have tea in Mrs. Halsey's tea shop. I have a cook and maid and groundskeeper to take care of all my needs."

"And what of the ghost?"

Brioc arched an eyebrow.

She took her brother's arm. "Help me climb the rest of the way up, and I will tell you all about him. He is a hero, did you know?"

"Does he really exist? Will he scare my little girls?"

"No, of course not."

"And what of me and Anne?"

"He will not harm you, either. I promise."

Her brother sighed. "And what of Ashbrook?"

She inhaled sharply. "Ashbrook? He came with you? Oh, Robert! Why did you allow it?"

Brioc growled softly. "I thought you said there was no one."

"There is no one," she shot back without thinking.

Her brother looked over his shoulder to where Brioc was now standing, two steps up from him. "What are you talking about, Hen?"

She frowned at Brioc.

He frowned right back at her. "Who the hell is Ashbrook?"

Chapter Six

"WHAT ARE YOU going to do, Hen?" Brioc paced across his bedchamber, eager to talk to her now that she had retired for the evening, and they had time alone. "Why did you tell me you had no one? The Earl of bloody Ashbrook is not exactly no one."

"He is a good friend of my brother's. Best friend, really. He does not love me. He is doing this because he thinks it is the honorable thing to do for my brother's sake. Did you see the slightest look of longing in his eyes?"

"Yes."

"You are just saying that because..." She turned to face him. "Are you jealous?"

Brioc folded his arms across his chest. "I am a ghost. How can I be jealous?"

"You would also have to love me, I suppose." She shook her head to dismiss the notion. "Trust me, he does not love me. I am doing him a favor by rejecting him."

"Hen, do you have any idea how truly beautiful you are?"

She sank onto the chair by the hearth and tucked her legs under her bottom. "Are you going to tell me again that you would have courted me had we met during one of my London seasons?"

"Why is it so farfetched?"

"Because you are too handsome for words. You are a sophisticated captain, and I am a wallflower. Can we please not have this conversation? You would have looked past me and never once noticed me. Just as Ashbrook did not notice me until my brother confided my situation to him. Suddenly, about two months ago, the man was having flowers delivered to me, horrid ones that made me sneeze because he did not think to ask me which ones I preferred or whether I had any particular sensitivity to them."

Brioc stifled a grin. "I did not ask you, either."

"You never had flowers delivered to me. But had I started to sneeze in the garden, you would have asked me about it. *What can I do for you, Hen?* That's what you would have said."

He settled on the ottoman beside her. "So you are going to reject him out of hand because you did not like his flowers?"

"I am going to reject him because he is in love with Lady Anissa Deverell, and she is in love with him. But he thinks this bond of brotherhood with Robert is more important than his own happiness. Besides, he thinks I will be dead before the year is out."

Brioc's breath caught in his throat. "Will you, Hen? Is this what your doctor told you?"

She nodded. "But wouldn't it be a jest on all of us if I lived another twenty years?"

Brioc said nothing.

He would wait for her. Twenty years. Fifty years. A hundred years.

Someone knocked lightly at her door.

She had settled her brother and his wife in a guest chamber down the hall and put the girls in a connecting room next to them since Anne was still nursing baby Chloe. The Earl of Ashbrook was also settled in a bedchamber at the other end of the hall.

They were all too far away to hear him and Hen chatting.

"Who could that be?" she grumbled, rising from her chair. She had changed out of her gown and into her nightrail and robe, going through her usual routine that he found so familiar and surprisingly comforting to him.

She opened the door cautiously, obviously surprised to find Ashbrook there.

Brioc cursed under his breath. "I am going to chase the bloody bounder out."

Hen cast him a frown, which he took as a plea to keep out of it.

"Why are you here, my lord?" she said with commendable indignation.

"Come now, Hen. Surely, we need not be so formal."

Brioc noticed that she clutched the door a little tighter.

He was going to flatten the bounder if he tried anything untoward with her.

"That begs the question. Why are you here?"

"Because we need to talk."

Hen stepped forward to block his entry. "Anything you have to say to me can be said tomorrow morning within my brother's hearing."

"No, this cannot. I need to know how you truly feel about me, Hen. You were infatuated with me as a little girl."

"But you never liked me, nor do you particularly like me now."

"That isn't true. I do like you. I can no more bear to see you suffer alone than your brother can. Why will you not accept to marry me? I can give you everything."

"Can you give me love?"

He blushed. "I...yes...if this is what you must have. You are Robert's sister...I can..."

"Stop, please. You love my brother, not me. I love him, too. He is a wonderful person, is he not? A true and loyal friend and the best brother a girl can have. Be a good friend to him when the time comes, but do not destroy your own life to accommodate his. What you need to do is grab your happiness with Lady Anissa. Do not be an idiot and delay proposing to her. Love is precious. Do not throw it away." She shoved him gently out the door. "You are a dear friend to us, but I want you gone first thing in the morning."

She shut the door in his face, then turned to Brioc. "I am going to stay here until I take my last breath. No one can make me leave, not even you. So don't you dare start haunting me. You will never chase me away."

"I like having you here, Hen. But are you being fair to your brother? He is mad with worry over you." He sighed and ran a hand through his hair, wanting to be possessive and keep her with him but knowing she would be better off with her loved ones around her.

He was a damn ghost.

No matter how desperately he loved her, he could do nothing to help.

"I don't want to return to London. The air is thick and dirty. I'll only sicken faster. And what of my sweet nieces? I don't want them to see me frail and helpless. I don't want that, Brioc. I want their memories of me to be happy, not sad and filled with pity."

"All right, Hen."

"So I will enjoy my week with them and then send them on their way." She walked to her bed, slipped off her robe, and settled under the covers.

Brioc worried about her when she curled up in a little ball and began to sniffle. "Hen, I'm coming into bed with you. I want to hold you in my arms. Is that all right?"

"It's your bed more than it is mine."

"Is that a yes?"

She nodded.

He was surprised, but she was hurting and probably willing to overlook the impropriety, since he was a ghost anyway and no one was going to see him. She had felt his kisses, but would she also be able to feel his arms around her?

He could not feel her.

Why had it only worked one way?

He wanted so badly to draw her body against his and feel the warmth of her skin against him.

He climbed in beside her and wrapped his arms around her.

To his utter surprise, he felt her.

"Can you feel my arms around you, Hen?"

She remained turned away from him so that her back was to his chest, and they were spooned together. "Yes."

"I can feel you, too."

She said nothing, just cried herself to sleep.

Come morning, Brioc was surprised to find himself still in bed with Hen, his big body half atop her and his hands cupping her in places he had no right to touch. He eased away, shaking his head in confusion as he rose and made his way to the balcony. It was almost dawn, and the familiar mist was rising off the water and hugging the flower beds. "Why am I still here?"

He turned to Hen in alarm. "Hen, wake up. Talk to me."

She grumbled sleepily and opened her eyes. "What's wrong? Why did you wake me?"

"I slept with you. Now, it is dawn, and I'm still here."

She sat up in surprise. "What does it mean?"

He sank heavily onto the bed. "I was afraid it meant...I thought you..."

"Oh, I see. No, I'm not dead. But it is most confusing. I see what you mean." She started to rise but turned him when they heard scratching sounds at the door. "Oh, dear. If that is Ashbrook, you are to do nothing, no matter what he says to me. I want your oath, Brioc."

"Damn it."

"Your oath."

"All right. But if he touches you, I will punch him."

"Aunt Hen," her namesake called through the door. "Who are you talking to?"

Her eyes widened.

Brioc laughed. "They can hear you, but not me. I'll stand on the balcony, out of the way."

She nodded. "I'm coming, my little chicks."

She opened the door to allow Henley and Phoebe in. They scrambled onto the bed beside her. "This side is warm, too," Phoebe said and snuggled where Brioc had been sleeping until moments ago.

Henley buried her head in the pillow. "It smells like the spiced rum Papa has every Yuletide. Then he and mama get all giggly, and he kisses her."

Hen laughed. "That's because he likes her."

"Is that man going to kiss you?" Phoebe asked, staring up at her with adorable, big eyes.

"Oh, you mean your papa's friend, Lord Ashbrook? No, my chicks. He is not going to kiss me. He is going home today."

Henley stared at the balcony. "No, not Papa's friend. That man, the one standing on the balcony with his arms folded over his chest."

"Blessed saints," Brioc muttered, stepping back inside. "You can see me?"

Both girls nodded.

Hen looked ready to faint. "Girls…it isn't…you cannot say a word to your papa…he…good heavens. Oh, dear. I cannot have them lie."

Brioc knelt beside the bed. "Phoebe. Henley. You must tell your father the truth, of course. But he may not believe you."

They nodded again.

"Because you are the ghost? We saw your portrait over the mantel in the parlor," Henley said. "Papa is afraid you will hurt Aunt Hen."

"No, I would never do that. I give you my sacred oath. I will always protect her and never harm her. You can tell your papa I gave you my sacred oath."

Which they did later that morning as Hen, her nieces, and brother and sister-in-law sat around the breakfast table. Ashbrook had left for London an hour ago, so it was just the family seated with her.

"Phoebe," Hen's brother said, his expression puzzled as he gazed at his daughter. "Who gave you a sacred oath?"

"The ghost, Papa," Henley replied for her sister. "He is ever so nice."

"He looks just like his portrait, but even handsomer," Phoebe said. "He promised never to hurt Aunt Hen. He said he will protect her."

Her brother and his wife exchanged panicked looks.

"My darlings, you saw the ghost?" Anne asked, her cheeks turning pale. She was dandling baby Chloe on her lap and now held her a little closer.

"Yes, Mama." Henley nodded. "So did Phoebe. He was by Auntie Hen's bed."

"I think he wanted to sleep with her," Phoebe added helpfully.

Hen snorted while struggling to hold back her laughter.

Her brother was not at all amused. "Hen, what are you putting in their heads?"

"Me? I have done nothing. They climbed into bed with me this morning. We had a lovely chat. We are going to walk down to the dock this morning and look at all the smelly fish. Aren't we girls?"

"Captain Arundel said he would join us," Henley said.

Robert set his fork down with a clatter. "Girls, I do not think it will be possible. Something urgent has come up, and I am afraid we must return home. Anne, kindly take our girls upstairs. Hen, I need to talk to you."

The girls began to cry, but Anne calmed them. "My loves, if you cry, then you will make baby Chloe cry. So do be good and put smiles on your faces."

Hen was now alone with her brother.

"They spend one night here and are already talking about the ghost, Hen. What is going on?"

"You knew about the ghost of Captain Arundel. He hasn't harmed me, nor will he ever harm your girls. But you are overset now. I told you not to bring them here, although I am glad to see them again. Stay the week. What harm is there now? They will love this place as much as I do."

"No. We must go. I will not have them dreaming about ghostly horrors. I'm sorry, Hen. You were right. I should not have brought them here. I will return by myself in a couple of months. In truth, you look well. Better than I ever saw you look in London." He rubbed a hand across the nape of his neck. "I'm also sorry I brought Ahsbrook."

She smiled wryly. "Well, some good came of it. He will now propose to Anissa. At least, I hope so. He is a fool if he doesn't. Will you talk sense into him, Robert? Love is a thing to cherish, never to be taken for granted."

"What of you?"

"I am happy here. You can see that I am."

"Yes." But he looked obviously pained. "I will return in two month. Write to me if you need anything."

"I will." She rose along with him. "I love you. You are the best brother in all of England."

"And you are the most irritating sister ever to exist." He drew her into his arms and hugged her. "I love you, Hen. Please take care of yourself. And come to me at once if you ever change your mind. You are always welcome to stay with us."

"I know."

But she did manage to spend a little of the day with her nieces, taking them to the smelly fish market and a stop for cherry pie at the tea shop before they packed up their coach and returned to London.

Brioc did not join them while they sauntered through the village, realizing it would only upset Hen's brother further if his girls started talking to him. The sooner the little ones forgot about him, the better.

By nightfall, the cottage fell quiet.

Brioc was waiting for Hen when she climbed the stairs to his bedchamber. She set down her candle and sank onto the chair by the hearth.

He sat beside her on the ottoman. "Hen, how are you holding up?"

She smiled at him. "A little tired, but nothing that a good night's sleep cannot cure. I do wish my nieces could have stayed longer. But I suppose it is for the best. We still have our puzzle to figure out."

"What puzzle?"

"You, of course. We still need to find out why you are bound to this cottage."

He took her hand, amazed that he could feel it wrapped in his. "We don't, Hen. I've figured it out."

Her eyes widened in surprise. "You have? Tell me. Is there something I can do to help free you?"

He rubbed his thumb lightly over the top of her hand, loving the delicate feel of her skin. "I am free. I have always been free."

"What do you mean?"

He leaned over and kissed her gently on the lips. "Did you feel that, Hen?"

She nodded. "You taste of the cherry pie I brought home from Mrs. Henley's tea shop."

He grinned. "It's my favorite. I couldn't resist."

"But I don't understand," she said, now frowning. "Why are you here if you claim you were always free?"

He caressed her cheek, marveling at its softness. "For you, Hen. I am here for you. By your side is where I belong for as long as you need me."

Her hand trembled. "For me?"

"I love you, my beautiful lass. I knew it the moment I set eyes on you. You came here with Mr. Priam, that arse of a land agent. I watched you walk through my home and then stroll through my garden. I suspected in that moment why I stayed, but I wasn't sure until now. It was for you. To hold you and love you forever."

Tears formed in her eyes. "I love you, Brioc. So very much. I did not think I could ever feel this way about anyone. My heart is yours for always. But…what happens now?"

"We wait."

"For me?" She put a hand to her heart. "It will happen soon, won't it?"

"Yes, love. This is why we are able to feel each other now. Don't be afraid, Hen. I will never leave your side. When you are ready, I will walk with you. Hand in hand."

"Are you sure I will not lose you?"

"Never, Hen. Our hearts are bound." He stood and brought her up with him. "Come, love. Come to bed and let me hold you in my arms."

"Will you take off your shirt?"

He grinned. "Only if you will take off your nightgown."

She cast him a loving smile. "I can be persuaded."

He took her in his arms and felt the sweet taste of her lips as he kissed her with all his heart and longing. "*Blessed saints*. I love you, Hen."

She smiled at him, her gaze soft and tender. "Who knew haunting could ever be this much fun?"

Also by Meara Platt

About the Author

Meara Platt is an award winning, USA TODAY bestselling author and an Amazon UK All-Star. Her favorite place in all the world is England's Lake District, which may not come as a surprise since many of her stories are set in that idyllic landscape, including her paranormal romance Dark Gardens series. Learn more about the Dark Gardens and Meara's lighthearted and humorous Regency romances in her Farthingale series and Book of Love series, or her warmhearted Regency romances in her Braydens series by visiting her website at www.mearaplatt.com.

Made in the USA
Columbia, SC
05 June 2025

59007196R00035